D0569765

Dear Parents:

Congratulations! Your child is taking the first steps on an exciting journey. The destination? Independent reading!

STEP INTO READING® will help your child get there. The program offers five steps to reading success. Each step includes fun stories and colorful art or photographs. In addition to original fiction and books with favorite characters, there are Step into Reading Non-Fiction Readers, Phonics Readers and Boxed Sets, Sticker Readers, and Comic Readers—a complete literacy program with something to interest every child.

Learning to Read, Step by Step!

Ready to Read   Preschool–Kindergarten
• big type and easy words • rhyme and rhythm • picture clues
For children who know the alphabet and are eager to begin reading.

Reading with Help   Preschool–Grade 1
• basic vocabulary • short sentences • simple stories
For children who recognize familiar words and sound out new words with help.

Reading on Your Own   Grades 1–3
• engaging characters • easy-to-follow plots • popular topics
For children who are ready to read on their own.

Reading Paragraphs   Grades 2–3
• challenging vocabulary • short paragraphs • exciting stories
For newly independent readers who read simple sentences with confidence.

Ready for Chapters   Grades 2–4
• chapters • longer paragraphs • full-color art
For children who want to take the plunge into chapter books but still like colorful pictures.

STEP INTO READING® is designed to give every child a successful reading experience. The grade levels are only guides; children will progress through the steps at their own speed, developing confidence in their reading.

Remember, a lifetime love of reading starts with a single step!

Step into Reading, Random House, and the Random House colophon are registered trademarks of Penguin Random House LLC.

Visit us on the Web!
StepIntoReading.com
randomhousekids.com

Educators and librarians, for a variety of teaching tools, visit us at RHTeachersLibrarians.com

ISBN 978-0-553-52203-7 (trade) — ISBN 978-0-553-52204-4 (lib. bdg.)

Printed in the United States of America   10 9 8 7 6 5 4 3 2 1

nickelodeon

SHIMMER and Shine™

Meet Shimmer and Shine!

by Mary Tillworth

illustrated by José Maria Cardona

Random House 🏠 New York

Meet Shimmer.

Meet Shine.

They are twin genies!

Shimmer and Shine
live in a genie world.

Shimmer hugs

her pet monkey, Tala.

Shine gets a lick
from her tiger, Nahal.

Shimmer and Shine

love their pets!

Today Shimmer
and Shine get
to grant wishes!
First they must make
a genie bottle.

They mix

a ray of sunshine

with sand

from the beach.

Shimmer adds
a drop of water
and a cloud.

Shine tops
the bottle
with a star.

The genie bottle
is perfect!

The Magic Mirror
shows the genies
a girl named Leah.
Shimmer and Shine
will grant her wishes.

Leah and her friend Zac
are at a carnival.

They see a game
they want to play.

Leah tosses a ring.

She wins a prize!

Leah picks
walkie-talkies
for Zac.

She is a good friend!

The man in the booth

lets Leah pick

a second prize.

Leah picks

a genie bottle necklace.

Inside a fun house,
Leah's necklace
begins to sparkle!

Shimmer and Shine
fly out of the bottle
with their pets!

The genies tell Leah
they can grant her
three wishes a day.

Leah wants
to tell Zac
about the genies.

Leah cannot tell anyone
about the genies.
If she does,
she will lose
them forever!

Leah promises
not to tell.
She cannot wait
to make wishes
with Shimmer and Shine!